"IT'LL BE FUN" HE SAID
by GLEN CRESSMAN

Copyright © 2021 by Glen Cressman.

First Edition
First Printing, 2021
ISBN: 9798722357939

Author: Glen Cressman
Editor: Kenneth Watts
Cover Art: Kenneth Watts (DKTR)
        Music: soundcloud.com/dktrdktr
        Visuals: etsy.com/shop/thedktr

All rights reserved. No part of this book may be reproduced, stored, transmitted, or otherwise copied for public or private purposes.

All persons, places, incidents and actions in this book are a work of fiction. Any similarity to real persons, places, incidents and actions is purely coincidental.

GLEN CRESSMAN

24 Huron St. W. P.O.Box 357
Thessalon, Ontario, CANADA
P0R1L0
705-542-9456
ratboybrown2@hotmail.com

ACKNOWLEDGEMENTS

To my friends and family who over the years have endured my seemingly endless stories from my past and encouraged me to write them down. I thank you.

To five special people, Simon Lacombe, Gayanne Bronicheski, Denise Perigord, Ellen Weatherbee and Hilda Doherty. Once I started this project it was not just their encouragement to finish what I started but their input to my endless questions on how to write an 18,000-word short story. Being a retired millwright didn't prepare me for the task.

To Ken Watts, my editor, cover designer and computer aid, without whose expertise I would never have published this book. I thank you.

DEDICATION

To the late Robert Fuchs. Have the sherry ready my friend.

Table of Contents

PRELUDE 1
DAY ONE 6
DAY TWO 14
DAY THREE 21
DAY FOUR 26
DAY FIVE 31
DAY SIX 37
DAY SEVEN 40
DAY EIGHT 47
DAY NINE 55
DAY TEN 59
CONCLUSION 72

PRELUDE

I've always been a daydreamer, thinking of out-of-the-ordinary ways to go through life's normal journeys. I still remember my grade six teacher shouting at me, "Gerald! Pay attention! Quit looking out that window, what's so damn interesting out there anyway?" I find most average peoples lives are usually remembered by the most interesting and memorable times from their past. Good and bad. Much like pages in one's book of life. A lot of my friends think I have a screw loose. Maybe so. But over the years I like to think I've been instrumental in adding many pages to theirs and my books. Mostly good, some bad.

I'm a 60-year-old recently widowed, recently retired tradesman who like a lot of my closest old friends have spent the last 30 years working at the local steel plant. My name is Gerald Crest (a.k.a. Batman, a.k.a. Gill).

Today however, I received a most unusual letter from a person I encountered a while back that has me, as my dad would say, not knowing whether to shit or wind my watch. The letter has no return address, is typed out, is addressed to me, and is without the name of the person who wrote it. However, I do know who sent this letter. This letter pertains to a recent page filled adventure I took with my old friend Fooch (a.k.a. Francis Feldman). I think it's best I read it to you after I tell you my story. It may make some sense to you then. Please bear with me. It's a good story.

This adventure started a few months ago about a week or so after we both retired from the steel plant. We were sitting at Fooch's kitchen table just shooting the shit. Kitchen tables seem to be a place where regular folks solve most of the world's problems. I had just explained to him my brilliant plan for the two us to visit another old friend, 'Nitty' who lived out west in

Edmonton. Nitty was nearing his retirement and is planning on moving back here to southern Ontario in the near future. Now you might say my buddy Fooch wasn't very receptive to my plan.

Fooch, "So let me get this straight, your brilliant plan is for the two of us to hitchhike across the country to visit Nitty in Edmonton, some 3500 km from here. You say 'remember the fun we had when we hitched to Silver Lake' way back when we were in our teens. As I recall that adventure took us ten hours to go 150 km including two hours in the back of a Mennonite buggy. Are you insane? Why don't we just drive out or take the bus? We're not flying out. You know how I hate planes."

Laughing I tell him, "Where's the fun in that? It will be different this time, we're older, wiser, have money, have no time frame to follow, besides we're running out of 'remember when'. Think of all stories we'll have to tell. I have a foolproof plan this time."

Reluctantly Fooch asks, "Okay genius what's your foolproof plan?"

I simply tell him, "Signs."

Fooch looks around in disbelief finally stares at me and shouts "SIGNS! What the hell does that mean?"

I quietly lay out my plan, "People are generally curious. People, especially women are leery of picking up hitchhikers. I understand that. We're 60 years old. The fear factor of picking up two old farts is lower at our age. We travel light, a backpack each and we carry a light case with our sign making materials in it. One of those white backing boards that you can attach magnetic letters to. That way we can change our sign any time to suit our situation. We take a little cash, credit cards, cell phone, change of clothes, tunes, and some refreshments. We make sure we get dropped off near towns so we can get lodging. Just remember what Doris Day would say."

Fooch still in disbelief, "Doris my ass, there's something seriously wrong with your head. Look at us. You look like a perverted old hippy and I'm an overage, overweight grizzly looking biker type. Who's going to pick us up? What if we get rolled or robbed. What if we get stuck in the middle of nowhere. What happens when the weather turns ugly? We're not 16 anymore

Fooch pauses for a moment. His first big mistake "How long do you think it would take us to go 3500 km? And how in god's name do you think these signs are our secret weapon?"

I'm smiling now "So your at least your thinking about it. Good. I figure it should take us at least a week maybe two. If it looks hopeless there's always plan B, we ride the Greyhound. Just trust me about the signs. I've been thinking about this for months. You worry too much. Look man we're running out of stories to tell, think of some of the people we will meet, maybe an adventure or two, hell maybe we'll get laid."

Fooch, "Yah, hopefully it's not by a guy named Bruno. I can't believe I'm even thinking about doing this. You've come up with some dumb ideas over the years. This one's right at the top of the list."

It's about 11 am. Fooch takes another haul from his bottle of cheap sherry. He always keeps a bottle wrapped in it's original brown paper bag. He drinks sherry because there's more bang for your buck. He hands me another beer.

"So, let's say we leave around July 1st. Avoid blackfly season. That's over two weeks from now so we have lots of time to get ready. Now we can't hitch on 400 series highways so we have to get past Barrie. After that we're home free."

"Home free my ass! Then we only have 3200 km to go. Brilliant."

"I've already got our first ride. Tamarack is heading up to his cottage in Collingwood the end of June. He's happily agreed to take us that far."

Fooch, "I'll bet he has the dink. What does he think of your brilliant plan?"

"Once he stopped laughing he was all for it. I talked to your daughter Sandra. She said she would gladly look after the house while we're gone. She said go, stay awhile."

"Yah yah, I'll bet she did. You know Gill, if your wife were still alive, god rest her soul, she'd say the same to you, go, stay awhile."

"So, it's settled then. We leave with Tamarack Thursday morning last day of June."

"Settled my ass! You're not joking, are you? How do you come up with these dumb ideas? Does Nitty know about this or are we going to surprise him?"

"Now my friend, speaking of dumb ideas, I talked to Digits a few days ago. Remember that dumb idea I came up with 35 years ago about our 'Wing' retirement home investment and the big busted blondes who'll be our caregivers? Well, it looks rather promising. He's looking into buying that old age home right out the old chicken hatchery road near the edge of town. The place is in financial trouble. He thinks it would suit our needs with a little renovation. You were at the last investment meeting, Christ we have over $700,000 in there."

Digits is another old friend from the neighbourhood. He never worked at the steel plant. He's a university grad with a degree in economics and in charge of the group's 'Wing' investment plan.

"Yah, yah, that was one of your better ideas I'll give you that."

"So, let's have a toast to Digits and all the big busted blondes that will look after us in our waning years at the 'Wing'."

DAY ONE

The two weeks since the kitchen meeting pass quickly. The guys are again at Fooch's place going over their gear for their adventure. The door bell rings. It's Tamarack, right on time. Fooch lets him in and they proceed to the kitchen where the gear is being inspected and packed up.

Tamarack has a huge grin on his face "So this is the beginning of 'Batman and Fooch's' great adventure."

Fooch "Why the hell do all you guys call him Batman. How the hell did you ever get that nickname anyway?"

"Nitty hung that on me years ago and for some reason it took. How does that bother you? "

"Well to me I'm still calling you 'Gill' or asshole, whatever the situation calls for."

Tamarack carefully inspects the gear. Utility knives, first aid kit, matches, lighters, flashlights, change of clothes, the whole nine yards.

"Looks like you're going camping. I see Fooch you have your pretty-up bag. What's this thing?" He holds up what looks like an art carrying suitcase like thing.

Fooch rolls his eyes "That's Gill's secret weapon."

"Oh, yah this is for your signs. Right, right." He lets out a laugh.

Fooch and Gill load their gear into Tamarack's SUV, grab some coffees to go and take off.

The weather forecast for the next few days looks good. The three talk about the joys and the drawbacks of retirement. Some people have difficulty having their routine changed and not seeing people that they've known and seen regularly for years. A drawback. They all agree though that one's expanding time-window is one of the best aspects of retirement. Not so much how much time you have left on the planet, but that you no longer have to say I can't go there or do that because you have to be to work on Monday. Things like that. About two hours later Tamarack drops Fooch and Gill off just outside of Collingwood at a busy intersection with a gas station, a Timmy's and a motel all within walking distance.

They say their goodbyes and from behind a huge grin Tamarack says "If you get into trouble before Parry Sound call me, past there you're on your own. Do you have the Greyhound number handy?"

Although he sounds half serious, you can tell he's enjoying the moment.

He starts to chuckle "Oh and by the way what does your first sign say?"

Gill shows him a sign reading simply 'Two Old Guys Looking for a Ride.' Fooch just rolls his eyes.

Tamarack shaking his head drives off.

It's about 11 am. Gill heads to Timmy's, refills his coffee and gets a few donuts. He returns to see Fooch taking a haul from his brown bag. The two take their stance at the side of the road and wait.

The guys have been patiently waiting for an hour or so. Several cars have honked and laughed at them.

Fooch laments "This is the dumbest idea you've ever had.

Why do I listen to you? I must be an idiot."

Just then a pink Toyota pulls over. Gill walks over to talk to the occupants. The passenger window rolls down. Gill looks in. There are two ladies in their 40's in the car.

The red head says "Nice sign. Where are you guys headed?"

Gill explains there headed out west but need to get past the 400 series of highways.

The red head then asks "Your buddy there, he looks a little scary. Is he okay?"

Gill explains he's just an old fart and is harmless. No worries.

Red head, "I'm Heather this is my sister Beth. We're going to Parry Sound. We can take you that far."

Gill smiling "That's great. We really appreciate it."

He prances back to Fooch "Yah see, it's the sign oh ye of little faith, the sign."

The guys load their gear into the backseat of the Toyota and off they go.

Again, Gill whispers to Fooch "It's the sign, remember the sign."

After they drive north for a while the 'Canadian Shield' slowly makes its presence known. Farmland begins to make way for thick bush and gradual rolling hills before the highway cuts through forest covered rock.

Beth, the driver who's rather attractive asks "Where out

west are you guys headed?"

Gill "If you must know we're going to surprise a friend in Edmonton."

"Are you shitting me! That's over 3000 km from here. Are you guys hurting for money? Why not just drive there? Take the bus. Fly out for god's sake."

Fooch "That's what I told this asshole. All except the fly out part." He then takes a haul from his bottle of sherry.

Gill explains to the ladies "Where's the fun in that? With hitchhiking, though risky, you will meet different people, get into interesting situations… and what's the worst that can happen? We're 60 years old, retired, what do we have to lose?"

Both ladies are smiling and kind of agree. "So, what do your wives think about this adventure?"

"We're both widowed, retired, not that it would matter. Our wives would have told us to go anyway, stay awhile."

"Sorry to hear that. So where are you going to spend the night?"

Fooch notices both ladies are smoking "Thank god you smoke."

He pulls out a rollie, just tobacco not pot. Fooch has always smoked roll-your-owns. He doesn't like pot. Always saying he wants to be drug free, although he's broken that pledge on a few occasions.

After he lights it Beth notes "I didn't think anyone smoked rollies any more. Can I have one?"

Fooch hands her one. Heather, the red head looks at Beth

then asks again "Well, where are you going to spend the night?"

Gill simply replies "We'll get a motel room and head out in the morning."

Beth, the driver looks at Heather, smiles then says "We have a cottage in the Sound, there's an extra room, why don't you guys spend the night there and we'll drop you off in the morning out on the highway."

Gill, who's always been shy and never been good with women, senses something.

"If it's not going to put you guys out, that would be great."

Beth then asks Fooch "What's that you're drinking from that brown paper bag of yours?"

"It's fine Canadian sherry. More bang for your buck, 20 percent."

She asks Fooch for a haul of it. Fooch passes the bag forward. After both ladies take a haul, Beth winces, "God, how can you drink that shit?"

For the next hour, the four joke and complain, without getting too political, about some of society's problems, the PC police and where the world seems to be headed. The rock cuts are getting higher and quite beautiful. The Canadian Shield is starting to dominate the landscape.

They soon arrive in 'The Sound', pull into the liquor store, pick up some beer, some coolers and sherry. They pick up chicken wings and munchies as well. Ten minutes later they arrive at the ladies' cottage. It's a well-landscaped bungalow with beautiful wood siding that backs onto a small lake. Gill gets out of the SUV and takes in the view.

"This is beautiful. How long have you owned it? "

Heather "It was left to us after our parents died. We've been coming here since we were kids."

Gill "Sorry to hear about your parents."

"Yah life's a bitch sometimes. They were killed in a car crash on that god damn highway out there a few years back. My sister and I come here most long weekends to hang out and party. You never know when your number's up. Come on in. I'll show you your room."

As the guys are putting their gear in their room they can't believe their luck. A great place to sleep, two arguably younger women to party with and it's only their first night. They soon join the girls at the kitchen table for wings and a few drinks. Fooch with his sherry, Gill with a beer and the girls have coolers of some kind. Everyone is smoking.

Beth "Let's not talk about politics or how we'd solve the worlds problems OK. So, why are you headed to Edmonton? You're going to have a hell of a time getting there."

Gill "A friend of ours has been working out there for years. He plans on retiring soon and move back to Kitchener. That's where we're from. We're retired now and thought we'd pay him a surprise visit. Besides we have a plan B. If things go for a shit, the Greyhound."

The group party on like old friends, laughing, telling stories from their past. One thing these two guys (like most men) are good at is partying and talking stupid. Inebriation is setting in.

Fooch with his eyes motions to Gill then says "Let's go outside for a leak." The two excuse themselves and head outside.

Fooch, "Look, look what Beth just gave me." He shows

Gill a little blue pill.

"Is this what I think it is? Christ, I haven't been laid in years."

"You haven't been laid in awhile, what about me!"

"What do I do now?"

"If you don't know by now give me that damn thing. Maybe, although I can't imagine why, she wants to screw a fat, greasy old biker." They both laugh and head back inside.

The guys sit back down at the table. Fooch takes a sip from his brown bag and lights another rollie. Beth looks at Heather turns to Fooch, takes the cigarette from his mouth, buts it out, grabs his hand then leads him into her bedroom.

Heather smiling, "Well there's another one off her bucket list. She's always wanted to screw a biker."

She takes a swallow from her cooler looks at Gill, "Don't get any ideas Gill. Screwing an old hippy is not on my list."

Gill, "Heather my dear, you don't know what you're missing. I would disappoint you like you've never been disappointed before."

"That's a line I've never heard before. Has it ever worked?"

Gill seemingly accepting the fact that tonight is not his night, again, and will likely end up fantasizing what might have been simply smiles. "No. This is the first time I've used it. Pretty lame eh?"

Heather with a sympathetic frown on her face hands Gill a blue pill. "Well old hippy Gill, disappoint me like you've never disappointed a woman before."

Like a little puppy Gill follows Heather into her bedroom.

DAY TWO

It's around 10 am the following morning. The weather looks good. As promised Beth and Heather drop our guys off at the highway heading north.

"Good luck you old farts. If you're back this way by Labour Day weekend look us up. Maybe we'll let you disappoint us again."

The guys wave goodbye. They both have huge stupid grins on their faces.

Fooch "You know something Gill, you never cease to amaze me. Maybe this isn't the dumbest idea you've ever had. What's the sign saying today? Please no sex. I'm too old and too tired." They both laugh like two school boys.

"No Fooch let's stick with what works. 'Two Old Guys Looking for a Ride'."

Two hours pass. There seems to be enough traffic but no ride yet. Several horn honks but no ride.

Fooch complains to Gill "My back is killing me. Next town were in I'm getting one of those folding type lawn chairs."

Just then a full-size van pulls over. Three scruffy looking young men, likely in their early twenties stop and open the side sliding door. Gill approaches the passenger window and eyes up the young men. The passenger window goes down.

The young man asks "Where are you old timers headed?"

"North. Sudbury and beyond. We just don't want to be dropped off in the middle of nowhere."

"Well hop in, we're going that far."

Gill is a little suspicious by the look of these guys but they get in the back of the van anyway. A ride's a ride.

The young men seem friendly enough as they engage in small talk with the guys. Gill can't help but notice several small outboard motors, a few new batteries and a small generator in the back of the van. He's seen this before. About thirty years ago on a weekend fishing trip with some buddies on this same stretch of highway his truck broke down. His group hitchhiked to the nearest town for help. The guys that picked them up in a van had several similar suspicious items in the back. They were friendly enough and dropped the group off at the nearest gas station. Gill and his friends determined later these guys were out doing a little cottage shopping. Hell, they could have been the fathers of this present bunch of characters.

The driver of the van today, known as Steel asks again. "Where are you headed?"

"Sudbury would be great, but Edmonton eventually."

"Edmonton! Well boys we're not going that far."

Fooch pulls a mickey of rye from his boot and offers the young men a drink. The three each take a haul. Steel, a tall thin lad with a scruffy beard, who appears to be the leader says "You old boys are alright. We're just out doing a little shopping." The three young men all laugh.

Gill realizing the men are thieves says, "Everyone has the right to make a living."

Fooch asks if it's alright if he can smoke. He pulls out a rollie. The man in the passenger seat they call Hammer shouts, "Is that what I think it is? Let's have a toke."

Fooch "Sorry guys it's just tobacco."

"Bummer."

The van continues north, suddenly Hammer in the front passenger seat shouts "Turn left here! Turn!"

The van turns and proceeds down the road a few miles eventually turning into a secluded long laneway.

Hammer shouts "This is it. My buddy tells me these folks don't come here till after Labour Day."

Hammer, who appears to be in his early twenties looks like the kinda guy who could handle himself in a fight and from some of the scars on his face looks like he's been in a few. They pull up to what appears to be a hunting camp. There's a nice shed behind the camp. Hammer and the third guy in the van, Olly, a scrawny frail looking kid in his late teens hop out crowbars in hand and attack the door of the shed. Minutes later they return with a nice Honda outboard motor with gas tank and a new Honda portable generator. They are both smiling from ear to ear as they throw the items into the back of the van. Hammer gives the driver 'Steel' a high five.

Fooch doesn't know what to think says nothing. Gill just rolls his eyes and keeps quiet.

Soon they're back on the highway again heading north. Roughly an hour later, about 20 miles from Sudbury the van pulls off the highway into one of those long pull overs for trucks and the like with porta-potties and several containers for garbage.

Gill whispers to Fooch "Grab onto both of our backpacks and be ready. We may have to leave in a hurry."

Gill has been eyeing up the van side sliding door where

Olly is sitting. The van comes to a stop. Hammer the tough looking burly fellow turns and says, "Well old timers, this is where you get off. By the way we want some gas money."

Gill calmly says, "Sounds fair, how much? How's 20 bucks?"

"No, how's about all your cash and those two nice backpacks."

Gill calmly replies, "So you guys are going to leave two old farts on the side of the road with no money and just the clothes on their backs. How nice. I'll bet your mothers would be proud."

Hammer continues to stare down Gill. "Olly, grab their money."

"Ok, Ok." Gill reaches into his pocket pulls out his wallet. He fumbles with it for a moment pulls out two twenties and throws them at Olly's feet. As Olly reaches down to grab the money, Gill gives him a hard shove. Olly rolls forward between the front seats. In one motion Gill unlocks the side door and slides it open. He and Fooch quickly exit the van with the backpacks firmly in Fooch's grasp.

Just then a station wagon full of young children pulls in and stops slightly behind our guys and the van. All the kids jump out and run to the porta-potties. Hammer opens his door and gets out screaming at the guys. He then sees the kids.

The driver seeing all the kids shouts to Hammer, "Forget it, lets go."

Hammer reluctantly gets back into the van and off they go leaving the guys standing.

Fooch is sarcastically smiling at Gill. "Well old buddy,

they still have our secret weapon case. What are we to do now?"

After travelling about 50 yards the side sliding door of the van opens and out flies the sign case.

Hammer shouts back "Good luck you old farts." The van quickly pulls away.

Gill and Fooch slowly walk towards their sign case.

"I'm glad we didn't have to fight them to keep our stuff, Steel and Olly we could have handled but that Hammer guy, he would have been trouble."

Fooch "One things certain, we couldn't have out run them."

They gather their sign case walk over to the bush line and find a fallen tree to sit on. Fooch pulls out his brown bag and takes a haul. Gill grabs it from him does likewise.

"How can you drink this shit?"

"This is fine Canadian sherry, show some respect." After a slight pause Fooch says "Okay genius, what now?"

Thirty minutes later the guys are back at the side of the highway again with their sign now saying "Two Old Guys Not Shopping Looking for Ride to Sudbury."

Not long after a car with an elderly couple pulls over. The passenger window goes down. A smiling older lady says "Nice sign. We're headed to Sudbury. Jump in. What do you mean not shopping?"

The guys just smile happily jump in "Ma'am, it's a long story."

The greater Sudbury area, is known throughout the mining industry as having the largest nickel/copper producing mines in 'North America'. The city is built on top of a rolling landscape of the Canadian Shield. The bush is small and sparse. In some areas, it appears like you're on another planet. Yet there's a strange beauty to it. It's home to the famous Sudbury Nickel and has a terrific attraction known as Science North.

Thirty minutes later the couple drops off Fooch and Gill at a busy intersection in Sudbury with everything they need within walking distance.

After several thank yous Gill sarcastically asks "Do you want some gas money?"

The elderly driver smiles "After what you told us about your last ride, here's $40. Please take it. I insist and good luck."

The guys reluctantly accept the money and walk to the nearest hotel/motel to book in. There's a liquor store close by, so they load up on what they need. They also stop, order a pizza and get some munchies.

A few hours later the boys are sipping on a drink and reflecting on their past two days.

"You know Gill, so far this adventure of yours has added more pages to my book than anything that has happened to me in the last five years. I must say you're an f-ing genius."

"So now you're saying I'm not f-ing insane. Thanks. I still can't get over that older couple insisting we take that $40."

Gill looks at his beer bottle as if it will give him an answer. "Man, life is strange."

Several seconds later he says, "I don't mean to change the subject, but did you see how that little prick Olly ended up in the front of the van. He did a half summersault and his feet were on the dash."

The guys burst out laughing.

"Let's have a toast to Olly, that scrawny little prick."

After the toast Gill calmly says "Settle down old friend we still have 3000 km to go. Now tomorrow, if we make it to the Soo we can hook up with our old buddy Smiler. He's turning 89 tomorrow. We have to plan something special for him."

"You didn't tell me it was Smiler's birthday, hell yah, we'll take him to the casino. Does he know we're coming or is it another surprise?"

DAY THREE

Bright and early the next morning, the boys, a little hungover, are out on the highway with their sign "Two Old Guys Looking for A Ride to The Soo." Fooch has purchased two folding lawn chairs form the nearby hardware store and is ready for some sitting time. The weather forecast is iffy. Expecting rain but not 'till late in the evening. Around 2 pm an SUV pulls over. Gill walks over and the passenger window goes down. They are a younger couple with a golden retriever in the back.

"If you don't mind sharing the back seat with a one year old golden retriever you're welcome to come along. By the way, that's a nice sign. We're going as far as St. Joseph Island."

The guys hop in. St. Joseph Island is a couple hours west and is only 50 clicks from the Soo.

Now the back seat is pretty crowded with the guys, their stuff and the dog. Fooch has always been a cat lover, not so fond of dogs. It's funny how animals seem to sense things like that. The young dog is all over Fooch from the moment he sat down. Licking his face and beard. Probably feasting on last nights pizza leftovers stuck in Fooch's long beard. Tail wagging 100 miles an hour. Priceless. Twenty minutes later the dog named Karl is asleep on Fooch's lap.

The guys relax and enjoy the beautiful scenery along what is known as the North Shore of Lake Huron. Through Espanola, Blind River, Iron Bridge, Thessalon, Bruce Mines, all the while catching beautiful vistas of the North Channel which is world renowned as one of the best places for fresh water sailing.

The couple pull over at their turn off to St. Joseph island and let the guys out. St. Joseph Island is a beautiful larger island, famous for its maple syrup, situated between the North Shore and

Michigan.

Thank yous and good lucks are exchanged. A light rain begins to fall.

The guys set up on the side of the highway sign out and some 50 km from the Soo. It's around supper time. The rain quickly intensifies into a downpour.

Gill mutters, "Well isn't this sumsing. The god damn weather man has lied again. Light rain my ass."

The downpour continues for 20 minutes. Gill is holding the sign case over his head while Fooch is just toughing it out trying to protect his rollie from the rain. The guys are soaked.

"Too bad you didn't buy a couple of umbrellas to go along with those lawn chairs oh wise one. That way we'd be comfortable and dry, you wiener."

Just then a big old empty logging truck pulls over and picks the guys up. The trucker, a rough looking character in his 30's, smiling says, "I couldn't let two old boys stand out there in the rain.

Nice sign by the way. Where are you guys headed?'

Gill replies, "To the Soo would be great, anywhere near the water tower would be fabulous."

"I'm headed on to Montreal River but I go right past the water tower, I'll drop you off close. My name is Will. People call me Bughouse."

"Thanks, Will, our buddy Smiler, who lives near the water tower will be happy to see us."

Will has a puzzled look on his face, "You guys know

Smiler? Smiler McCabe?"

"Hell yah. Do you know him?"

"Hell yah! I'll drop you off right at his front door. My dad and gramps used to work with him. That guy is the most interesting person I've ever met."

The next 30 minutes are filled with stories about this Smiler fellow and his life. Smiler worked for the railroad for thirty some years before retiring and building a summer camp on a remote island in the North Channel where he once worked. He's a collector of railroad memorabilia and other historical items. His house and garage are filled with the stuff. It's like a museum. Beautiful.

About an hour later the trucker pulls up at Smiler's driveway. It's getting dark and rather warm outside. The rain has stopped. Will, Fooch and Gill get out of the truck and walk to the side door. Our guys are still wet as Fooch rings the side doorbell.

Fooch begins to whine, "He doesn't even know we're coming. What if he's not home?"

Moments later a sleepy-eyed old gent comes to the door wearing only boxer shorts and a bath robe."

"Well look what the cat dragged in."

Fooch greets him with a big bear hug, "How are you doing you old fart? We've come for your birthday."

He hands Smiler a bottle of double malt scotch. Smiler happily accepts the bottle then recognizes the truck driver, "Bughouse, what brings you here. How's your dad?"

Will with a huge smile on his face, "He's doing fine. You're looking good Smiler. Happy birthday" and shakes

Smiler's hand.

"I left my truck running so I can't stay but it was nice seeing you. Small world ehh, look who I picked up hitchhiking."

Fooch, "Bughouse? That's what they call you? How in god's name did you get that handle?"

Smiler says goodbye to Bughouse then looks at the guys, "You're all wet."

Smiler always the gracious host says goodbye again to Bughouse and invites the guys in. They immediately strip out of their wet clothes and put on just dry boxer shorts. All three wearing only boxer shorts then sit at the kitchen table. Smiler sets the bottle of scotch on the kitchen table accompanied by three glasses and a small pitcher of water. Double malt scotch happens to be Smiler's drink of choice. Shots are poured. It's said one has to acquire a taste for scotch, that's something Gill has never acquired.

"How can you two enjoy this crap?"

Fooch, "Just sip it, follow my lead. It's not a beer for Christ sake."

The three raise their glasses, "Lets have a toast, here's to two old farts and one real old fart, may the lord take a liking to us."

Fooch and Gill recount the first two days of their trip to Smiler. They still can't get over the coincidence of being picked up by this Will fellow and his connection to Smiler. Smiler just quietly smiles and shakes his head. He's very skeptical with the guys getting laid story but that aside is happy to see them.

"Let me take your wet clothes downstairs and throw them in the dryer."

Fooch, "Sit down Smiler, stop being our mother. Gill can do that."

Gill, "No problem, you wouldn't know how to turn the damn machine on anyhow."

Moments later, Gill returns from the basement. They have a few more shots.

Fooch then states, "Tomorrow we're taking you to the casino for your birthday. I have a foolproof plan. It's called double up quad. Can't miss. We'll win just enough money to buy Chinese food and more scotch. If it fails we come home with some Big Macs and soda."

Smiler quietly laughs. After a few more drinks the guys escort Smiler off to his bed, tuck him in and say goodnight.

The guys then wander from the kitchen into the living room gazing at the numerous curios and collectables beautifully displayed throughout.

"You know something Gill, over the years I've met a lot of your new friends and most of them are dinks, but Smiler is unique. I've only known him 10 years. I remember you telling me once you have old friends and new friends. Not new old friends. Sorry to say, but I consider Smiler a new old friend."

"Well Fooch old friend, I'm going to bed and sleeping till noon. Your new old friend has a cot ready for you in the basement beside the furnace. Goodnight. Don't forget to buy two umbrellas tomorrow."

DAY FOUR

The next morning, around 10 am Gill crawls out of bed and wanders into the kitchen to see Smiler making breakfast. He sees Fooch outside having a smoke. Smiler has few rules but one of them is no smoking in the house. Gill joins Fooch. They slowly walk around Smiler's yard and go into his garage.

Fooch, "Look at all this, it's beautiful. What do you call those trees with the big nobs on them?"

Gill, "They're burrows I believe."

"Well they're gorgeous."

"Ok Fooch, what's your big plan for today?"

"While you were still sleeping I spoke with Smiler. You know Gill you don't handle liquor very well anymore. As for today, the plan is Smiler is going to take us on a tour of the Soo, including a stop at the VV boutique and the 'Bushplane Museum'. Then around supper time we hit the casino."

The Soo is a beautiful city stuck between Lake Superior and The North Channel of Lake Huron. It's one of the oldest settlements in Canada. Home to the famous Soo locks, huge international bridge, famous Agawa Canyon railway run, huge steel mill, Bushplane Museum and lots more, including a great used clothing store the guys call the VV Boutique. The casino is right downtown. The guys soon join Smiler in the kitchen and have some breakfast.

Shortly after noon, the three start out in Smilers minivan for the guided tour. First stop is the VV Boutique. Fooch finds a pair of men's high cut dress shoes. Gill gets his hands on a long sleeve camouflage t-shirt while Smiler hunting in the knickknack section finds a brass bell. After a brief argument on who got the best deal they head downtown to the Bushplane Museum.

Smiler is a member so the guys get in for free. They spend a good hour there looking at the variety of restored bushplanes and even get to witness a 'Beaver 109' with pontoons land on the St. Marys River right in front of the museum. Very cool. They leave the museum, drive a few miles along side the St. Mary's River and park at the Soo locks right under the International Bridge for refreshments.

It's a beautiful afternoon. Fooch, well into his sherry, begins to explain his casino plan.

"It's called double up quad. At the roulette table, we pick a colour. Let's say we pick red."

Gill, "Why roulette? The odds suck."

"Forget it. I'm not going to explain it to you, asshole. When we get there just shut up and follow my lead."

Smiler who isn't drinking just smiles shakes his head and laughs. He has a unique low quiet laugh.

Gill, drinking a beer, "I know that game. You realize Fooch, if we lose we're down $300."

"Quit being such a downer. The odds are with us. Trust me. Have I ever let you down before? Follow my lead."

Gill smiling, "You haven't let me down today as yet. When are you going to buy those umbrellas?"

At the casino, our threesome has been playing this double up quad for a couple of hours now and are up only $40. Once they had to bet three red in a row, $80, just to get their money back. At the bar, they're taking a break. Fooch is bitching about the pricey wine he's having. Gill is nursing a beer. Smiler is having a coffee.

Fooch downs his wine, "Come on Gill, lets go get em."

They go to the roulette table and watch three black show up in a row. Fooch puts $20 down on red. Black comes up. He puts $40 down on red. Black comes up again. Fooch looks at the ceiling shakes his head puts $80 down on red. Black again.

"Are you shitting me!"

The handler quietly says, "Sir please keep your voice down."

Fooch by now is pretty much pissed. He only has $100 of chips left. He asks Gill to throw in the remaining $60 in chips to make the $160 bet. At the precise moment Gill pushes his chips onto red with Fooch's chips the handler says all bets down. It comes up red. Fooch is dancing about with glee.

"Finally. Chinese food and more scotch."

The handler proclaims, "I'm sorry sir, your bet was made too late" and pushes all the chips back.

Fooch's glee quickly turns to anger, "What the hell are you talking about? The bet was made! What the hell are you trying to prove?"

The handler, taken aback by Fooch's outrage, is looking around for help.

"Sir the bet was made too late, it's my call. Please take your chips and keep your voice down."

Gill quietly says, "With all due respect sir, the bet was made on time. Go to your camera. Go to the damn camera."

"Sorry fellas but it's my call."

Fooch snaps, "Well it's the wrong fucken call. What kind of operation do you bastards run here?"

Seconds later, four rather huge security guards approach the table.

The biggest one says, "Sir, you're going to have to leave the casino. Now!"

Fooch, "But they screwed us!"

A crowd of mostly older people are starting to gather. This kind of thing doesn't happen here very often.

Fooch is still furious, "Gill I'm going to hit one of these pricks" and walks towards the closest security guard.

Gill sizing up the situation quickly stands between the two.

"Easy Fooch easy. Look at the size of that guy. Think about it. Jail. Court case. Is it worth it? Let's just go. We'll get our money back another time."

Fooch still furious starts shouting, "They screwed us. These pricks screwed us."

Moments later our threesome is being escorted out of the casino and into the parking lot. Poor Smiler doesn't know what to think. Fooch is cursing the entire time. As they approach Smiler's minivan, Gill notices several yards back a casino security van following them. He abruptly stops, turns around and walks directly to the van. The driver side window slowly goes down.

Gill, "Look, I know you know we've been drinking. Our old friend here hasn't. If he drives us out of here can we go without being hassled?"

The driver of the van turns up his window and gets on the radio for a moment. He soon rolls his window down.

"Okay. If the old guy drives we'll let you go. Also tell your big friend he's banned from this casino for a year."

About an hour later, after stopping at McDonalds, the threesome is sitting at Smiler's kitchen table. Three Big Macs and three large orders of fries. Fooch pulls out a mickey of whiskey from his boot. Smiler calmly gets out three glasses then pours a good shot for each.

He quietly chuckles, "So, I guess the next time you visit we'll have the Chinese food. But I do love these fries."

Fooch is still furious, "Smiler, I know you're not a fan of cursing but those fuckers screwed us. This isn't over. We'll be back."

DAY FIVE

Next morning at 9 am, Fooch and Smiler are sitting at the kitchen table. Smiler has made a nice breakfast. Moments later Gill slowly walks to the kitchen table where Fooch and Smiler are talking.

Gill mumbles, "I have to learn to stick to beer."

Fooch smiling, "Yes you should. You look like shit."

There's not much talk about the previous night's events. It appears the guys are set on the task at hand. Hitch hiking to Edmonton. The local radio station has just announced it's National Zombie Day today. Really? What next?

Gill informs Fooch that the stretch from the Soo to Thunder Bay may be the toughest. It's some 400 miles with few big towns in between. In hitchhiking lore, it's been well known to be the worst section for hitchhiking in all of Canada. Smiler has agreed to take the guys just north of the Soo, but still close enough to civilization just in case.

They leave Smiler's via his minivan and stop at the local Walmart. Fooch, buys two umbrellas. Smiler drops the guys off, grins and says good luck. Todays sign reads 'Thunder Bay Would Be Nice'.

The guys set up at the side of the highway. After sitting in their nice new lawn chairs for over two hours, a half-ton truck stops. The driver says he's going as far as Montreal River which is about an hour north. The guys take the ride out of boredom and are let off in Montreal River. It's a nice little town, but not much there. They start to argue about the sign.

Gill finally says, "Put what ever the hell you want on the

damn thing. I'll take your lead. After all what could go wrong?"

Fooch reconfigures the sign 'Old Guys Looking 4 Adventure'.

Montreal River is a beautiful little town with a gorgeous view over looking Lake Superior. The guys have been enjoying that view in their lawn chairs for another three hours.

"Well Fooch, maybe we should think about looking for a place to stay for the night or at least think of changing the damn sign."

Before Fooch can reply a long, oddly painted van pulls over by the guys. It reminds Gill of a hippy type van he owned in the 70's, but this one is painted different. Tombstones, skeletons, set in a graveyard and the like. Quite striking. Very well done. Gill walks over to the passenger door. The window goes down. He's taken aback. A beautiful young lady made up like a zombie asks, "You two look like a couple of lost old zombies, so your looking for adventure ehh, want a ride?"

Gill manages to respond, "Yah, sure. Where are you going?"

"To Wawa, to the big zombiefest tonight. Hop in."

The guys cautiously get into the van. There's at least ten people all made up zombie-like partying in the back. The smell of pot fills the van.

The driver shouts "Hey Carrie, get your make-up kit out, it won't take much to make these two look like us."

The back of the van erupts in laughter. When your old and kind of desperate, insults like this don't mean shit. The guys are moving again heading north.

Fooch, "Hold off on the make up. Would any of you young zombies like a shot of whiskey?" He hauls his mickey out of his boot.

Someone says, "Welcome aboard. Give me a haul."

Despite the age difference, Fooch and Gill seem to fit right in. The guys find out that most of this gang are college students. They're skipping classes tomorrow in order to take part in the big zombie walk this evening. A few hours later the van lets the guys off in downtown Wawa.

Wawa is another beautiful town in the north. Famous for the humongous goose statue and beautiful lakes in the surrounding area. Although there are several motels in town they all seem to be booked for this zombiefest thing.

Gill, "Zombies. God damn zombies. Well isn't this sumsing."

Fooch, "Now what, asshole?"

"Why is it when we run into a slight problem I'm an asshole? Let's go to that restaurant over there, get something to eat and ask around. We're bound to find a place to stay."

After a feed of delicious chicken wings, they explain their situation to their waitress, Melanie, who promptly calls over one of the cooks from the back. The cook tells the guys he has a second-floor room he'll rent them beside the arena. It has an attached small balcony where they can smoke. Not fancy, but clean.

Gill, "Perfect, we'll take it."

After a short walk to the liquor store they pick up some booze and then some munchies. They soon find their room. It's in a very old house in rough shape. The cook's mother greets the guys at the side door. She gives them quite a long look-over before slowly, very slowly, letting them in and leading them up the stairs to the room. She has to be in her eighties. She tells the guys she was born in this house and will die in this house. Says if you smoke do it on the balcony, the toilet is down the hallway and no pissing off the balcony. Not fancy is an understatement. The balcony is quite small. It has a great view of the side entrance to the arena some 50 feet away.

It's a beautiful July evening, warm, very light breeze and no bugs. This time of year it doesn't get dark till around 10 pm.

"You know Gill this is a pretty little town, Canadian Shield mountains, beautiful lakes and you get us a place with a spectacular view of the arena."

Gill smiling shakes his head slowly from side to side, "You know something Francis, I love you but I've never met a man who bitches, about almost anything, as much as you do. Could you please go inside grab some munchies, bring me a beer, come back out and enjoy the show."

"What show?"

"Just do what I ask."

As Fooch heads inside he fails to notice the activity down around the arena side entrance. Special lighting is being setup and there appears to be a Sault Ste. Marie TV unit setting up their cameras.

Fooch emerges from the house onto the balcony with drinks and munchies.

"What's this show your talking about? You going to take your clothes off and dance around on the roof again?"

"I was ten years old last time I did that. No, you idiot, look down there."

Slowly coming from around the front of the arena are zombies. Dozens of them. The waitress at the restaurant had told Gill the zombie walk was starting downtown and culminating at the arena. Big party and dance to follow.

Cameras start flashing, a local TV reporter appears to be interviewing one of the organizers.

Fooch smiling now, "This is better than watching it on TV. Did you know this was going to happen?"

"I'm not just fog over here." Gill recognizes Carrie from the van and shouts down, "Hey Carrie, up here, you look damn fine dead."

She looks up at the balcony and still in her zombie character gives a zombie like wave. The guys cheer with delight. The cameraman notices them, pans up to the balcony and films the guys for at least 30 seconds. They pathetically attempt to act like zombies groaning, slurring words, failing miserably. The TV camera pans back to the entrance and follows the zombies inside. M.J.'s 'Thriller' is playing.

Gill, "Come on, lets go down there."

"Screw that. You go. I'm comfortable right here. Besides, there will be zombies coming out again from time to time and we can heckle them."

"Now how do you know that?"

"You know Gill sometimes you really are dumb. You see that sign above the door. 'NO SMOKING'. Today's zombies smoke. Just wait."

Sure enough, within 20 minutes a group of zombies come

out and they all light up. Mostly cigarettes.

Fooch, "I'm not just fog here you know."

The guys continue to drink and exchange reasonably polite banter with the zombies down below for quite some time. Fooch notices Gill has passed out in his chair. He walks over and gives him a slap.

"Come on you old fart. Let's get some sleep. We have to get out on that highway tomorrow and hit em hard."

DAY SIX

The next morning the guys grab some breakfast and then take the ten-minute walk out to the highway. Its about 10 am. The temperature is already close to 30 degrees. It's going to be a hot day. Today's sign again says, 'Thunder Bay Would Be Nice.' There's virtually no traffic heading north. Only a few transport trucks and a few tourists pulling campers.

Around 1 pm Gill says, "Let's change the sign. Any thoughts oh wise one?"

Fooch ignoring the comment simply says, "My ass is killing me."

A few moments later Gill shows Fooch the new sign. 'MY ASS IS KILLING ME'. Fooch just shakes his head and takes a haul from his brown bag.

He starts to whine, "Did you bring any ice? This shit is warm. What the hell are we doing out here?"

In the distance Gill sees the zombie van pull onto the highway heading south.

With a pathetic wave he says, "Bye bye Carrie. Man, that was some handsome woman. I'd sure like to disappoint her."

"You know Gill there's something seriously wrong with your head."

Hours later, around 5 pm, it's some 30 plus degrees with bright sunshine. The kind of weather you should be sitting on a nice sandy beach. Fooch is fast asleep on his lawn chair with brown bag on his lap. The new sign has generated little more than a few air horn blasts.

"Well isn't this sumsing. Come on you old fart. Wake up."

The guys decide to call it a day. They slowly stagger back to town and book into a motel.

After a quick cold shower, they head to the nearby restaurant, the same one they were at yesterday to grab some grub.

Fooch, "Well that was fun. What now genius? Time for plan B."

"Quit your damn whining. So we had a rough day. Shit happens. We'll come up with something. Have faith."

They both look up and see the local news is on the big screen TV above the bar. There's a segment on last nights zombie walk. Ironically it showing the guys on the balcony for about 15 seconds.

Melanie, the same waitress they had yesterday comes over, "Hey isn't that you two? Look everyone we have a couple of celebrities here. Can I have your autograph?"

The guys, smiling now, just roll their eyes. Moments later a large trucker type guy, named Bruno approaches their table. The type of guy you wouldn't want to mess with.

Fooch whispers to Gill, "This looks like the Bruno I was talking about."

Bruno asks, "Aren't you the two fools out on the highway today with that sign 'Thunder Bay Would Be Nice'?"

Smiling Gill replies, "Yah yah that be us."

"No one goes that far north from here. Try for White River

or Marathon."

He turns, looks at someone across the room and shouts, "Hey Hector, get your ass over here. Aren't you going to Marathon tomorrow? Why don't you give these old farts a ride? After all, they're celebrities."

Most of the patrons are now laughing.

Hector, a slim man in his late twenties approaches the guys. He looks more like a banker than a trucker.

Smiling he says, "I'll give you a ride tomorrow morning, but first you have to tell me what the hell your doing hitchhiking at your age way out here."

Bruno and Hector join the guys at the table. Fooch orders a round of drinks. Gill proceeds to tell them the whole Edmonton bound surprise an old friend, looking for adventure story.

Bruno, "Why wouldn't you fly out or at least take the 'Greyhound'? What are you stupid?"

Hector, "No. No. It sounds like an interesting undertaking. They're looking for adventure. I'm sure they'll find some. I'll take you guys to Marathon. It's not Thunder Bay but it's a step in the right direction. Be in front of this restaurant at 7 am. I'll be in the red Kenworth."

Hector and Bruno head back to their table. Bruno laughing gives Hector a friendly slap on the back and almost knocks him over.

"You see Fooch, oh ye of little faith, things have a way of working out. You have to learn to follow my lead."

"Yah, yah oh wise one. I'll tell you one thing, I'll not follow you out to that highway and sit for another eight hours. My ass is still killing me."

DAY SEVEN

As planned the guys meet Hector at 7 am in front of the restaurant and board his truck. It's a new unit with a sleeper and is hauling a flat bed trailer with a big-ass frontend loader on it. Gill crawls into the sleeper with their gear, Fooch is in the passenger seat.

Hector, "Get comfortable guys, we'll be several hours." Fooch asks if he can smoke. Hector, "Yah okay, just turn your window down a bit but don't throw the butts outside. There's a fire ban on."

Fooch pulls out a rollie and lights up.

"You guys are old school, could I try one of those?"

The group exchange small talk for awhile when Gill finally remarks, "You don't look or talk like your typical trucker. If you don't mind me asking what's your story? You and your buddy Bruno seem look like the 'odd couple'."

Hector, "I've known Bruno since my teens, he's real, he's honest and always says what on his mind. You see, I was born and raised in the Toronto area. I had a favourite uncle who lived up here. I'd be sent up here every summer to stay with him while my parents fought about money and what they wanted my future to be. It took only a few summers to realize I wanted to live up here and at the age of nineteen I quit college, left home and moved to Wawa to work at my uncle's garage. My father damn near flat-lined. That's where I met Bruno. He worked for my uncle. We had two things in common, we liked to work on machines and we loved to fish. The rest we just worked out."

He takes a drag on his rollie and continues, "Up here I've learned more about real people and life in general than I would have back home in a life time. People in these small towns help each other out, not just for money but say for, you know, I do for you, you do for me. There's a greater sense of community. Besides, up here if you screw somebody in business or pleasure for that matter the whole town knows."

A moment later Hector asks, "How long have you guys been on the road? Has it worked out?"

Smiling Gill replies "Well Hector let's see, this is day seven of our excursion, we've gotten laid, gotten robbed, gotten screwed at the casino, met some very interesting people and became celebrities at a zombie walk. You know just your normal hitchhiking stuff and just think we only have 1500 miles to go. We haven't been thrown in jail yet. So Fooch, what do you think, has it been worth it?"

Fooch, "Well genius, I've been looking at the map and this 'Marathon' place is again in the middle of nowhere. I'll be damned if I'm going to sit on the side of the road all day again and end up in the same place we started."

"Quit your bitching, has it been worth it?"

"I'm not saying it hasn't been worth it, I'm just saying- "

Gill interrupts, "Well what's your damn problem then?"

They continue to argue on like two old fools fighting over the last chicken wing on the plate. Hector has a huge grin on his face and it's apparent he likes the company of our guys.

They pass White River and head through some of the most beautiful Canadian Shield in the north.

Seemingly out of the blue Hector asks, "Do either of you have an AZ or AG license?"

Gill pipes up, "Yah I do. I used to drive truck way back. Why do you ask?"

"I have a friend in Marathon that owns let's call it a hotshot delivery service. He's always looking for drivers, especially for trips west. I sense you guys are trustworthy. Would you consider making a run for him? Think about it, I'll talk to him and see what I can do."

It's about supper time. The rig pulls into a large truck stop on the TransCanada highway a few miles north of the town of Marathon. The parking lot is crowded with rigs hauling all kinds of equipment. Mining, logging, general construction, you name it. It has a large restaurant/bar, convenience store, liquor store and motel.

"Here's a thought guys, why don't you get a room, get something to eat and I'll meet you back here in the restaurant in a few hours. I have to drop this loader off at the mine just north of here. In the meantime, I'll get in touch with my friend 'Milty' and see if he has a run going west."

"Sounds like a plan Hec. See you in a few hours."

Gill and Fooch leave the rig, wave and head to the motel.

A few hours later the guys are in the restaurant at a booth having supper. It's an older style truck stop restaurant, crowded with trucker types, a few locals and tourists because it's tourist season. There's a big screen TV behind the bar. At each booth are those old-style juke box selection card contraptions. You remember, you page through the cards, three songs for a dime, you punch in the song number. The song selection has been upgraded but still has many oldies on the cards. Well now it's three songs for a loonie. Fooch slides in a loonie then selects an old Patsy Cline song, 'I Fall to Pieces' followed by 'On the Darkside' by the 'Beaver Brown Band'.

"Ok Gill, I know you have no taste when it comes to music but you can have the last pick."

Gill secretly punches in the numbers for his song and smiles.

Moments later Hector and this Milty person join the guys in their both. Introductions are made. A waitress comes over. Hector orders a round of beers.

"Fellas you're in luck. Milty here has an overdue delivery to Saskatoon and no driver. I told him you have your AZ license and used to drive rigs way back, as you put it."

Just then the song 'I Fall to Pieces' starts playing.

Hector, "Who put that crap on?"

Before Fooch can reply Milty pipes up, "Crap! Are you shitting me, that's Patsy Cline for Christ sakes. Hector your taste in music is up your ass."

Fooch, "Yah, what he said."

Gill is quietly enjoying the argument. He then asks about the run to Saskatoon.

Milty explains the delivery vehicle is just a biggish cube van carrying two Harleys. Nothing difficult. A father and son were on a vacation travelling across the country when the father had a heart attack near here. The trip was cancelled and the two flew back home to Saskatoon. Through Milty's connections he was contacted and tasked with the job to return the bikes back to the family farm.

"If you accept the job I'll give you directions, contacts, expense money for gas, meals, motel etc. I'll also pay you $200 on delivery."

"We accept. How far is Saskatoon from here?" Gill reaches across the table and shakes Milty's hand.

"It's just over 1000 miles. What does your buddy think of the idea?"

"Screw him and the horse he rode in on."

Milty smiles, "Great, waitress another round of beers please."

Gill notices two young girls, around ten years old giggling and staring at him and Fooch.

One manages to gather up the courage to ask, "Aren't you the guys we seen on TV last night?"

Gill looking at Fooch sarcastically grins, "Yes, that was us. Do you want his autograph?"

The girls both scream with delight and take off back to their table.

Gill looks at the ceiling, "Please God, don't let this be my 15 minutes of fame."

Gill's song selection 'Sweet Hitchhiker' by CCR starts to play.

Hector smiles, "Now there's a song."

Milty, "God damn long hairs."

There's a sense of comradery between the group almost like a reuniting of old friends. They keep the beers, wine and songs coming. After a brief back-and-forth over country versus rock music, the general discussion turns to the guys seven days on the road adventure. Milty seems particularly interested with the idea of the hitchhiking signs the guys have used.

"Hector tells me you had a sign saying 'My Ass Is Killing Me'. Seriously?"

Gill feeling no pain, "Yah, that's right and still you pricks wouldn't pick us up."

Fooch, "You see what I have to put up with. There's something seriously wrong with his head."

Have you ever noticed the more men drink the louder and stupider they get?

Hector, "No Fooch I think your wrong. What you guys are doing is a fantastic idea. Look what you've experienced so far. Think of all the new pages you can put in that book you guys talk about."

Fooch with a sarcastic smile, "This coming from a guy who thinks 'I Fall to Pieces' is crap."

Now it's Milty's turn, "Yah, you god damn long hair, what he said." He reaches across the table and exchanges a high five with Fooch.

Milty, "Did you guys ever think of bringing a woman along to help with getting picked up? I mean, signs aside, no offence but look at you two."

Fooch, "We have feelings you know. Gill's thought of that. He has one deflated and rolled up in his backpack. She's for emergencies only. Unfortunately, Gill's portable air compressor isn't working."

The four howl with laughter. Drinking and talking stupid. It's a skill most men have mastered.

After a few more drinks the guys slowly stagger back to their motel room.

DAY EIGHT

As promised from last night, Milty meets the guys in the restaurant at 8 am. Fooch and Gill have just finished breakfast. Milty produces a file with the trips itinerary.

"The cube van is right out front; the bikes are loaded and secure. Here's the address with directions on where to deliver the bikes. It's at a farm just outside of Saskatoon. The McCaffrey Farm. Here's the address and directions where to drop off the cube van when your finished. It's at a friend of mine's business in the town. There's also some contact numbers if you run into any problems. And finally, here's your expense money. Please keep all the receipts and leave them in the glove box."

He hands Gill the envelope, "Well let's go out and have a look at this van of yours and the load it's carrying."

Out of habit from his trucking days Gill does a walk around, checking out the van and inspecting how secure the load is. In the back are two newer, beautiful black 'Harleys', lots of chrome and impressive saddle bags.

"Aren't these the centennial edition? Man, those are fine looking machines. How's the father doing anyway?"

Milty, "From what I've been told he had two stints put in and is recovering nicely. They plan on doing the trip again next year. Listen Gill, there's no panic on this delivery. Take your time. I just need it to get there. With any luck, you should make Dryden or even Kenora by day's end."

He hands Gill the keys then walks over to Fooch.

Fooch smiling gives him a hug and shouts, "Patsy Cline rules. Down with the hippies."

Moments later the guys are on their way, heading west. Most people who have taken a trip along the north shore of Lake Superior via The TransCanada Highway never forget it. It offers some of the most beautiful scenery one could imagine. High rolling Canadian Shield with awesome views of Lake Superior.

Not more than a couple of hours into their trip Gill notices the engine temperature gauge has risen and can detect a slight antifreeze odour.

"Houston, we may have a problem. Look for a safe place to pull over."

Within a few minutes they see an old abandoned motel near a town called Dorion and pull over. As Gill lifts the hood, a significant amount of steam is seen coming off the engine.

"Well isn't that sumsing."

Fooch looking down at the engine, "What now oh wise one? You're a millwright, can you fix it?"

As the steam leak dies down Gill can see where it's coming from, "The damn hose clamp on the top rad hose is partially broken. Son of a bitch."

"Can you fix it? Here we are again in the middle of nowhere. What now oh wise one?"

"We have to let this thing cool down. In the meantime, walk over to that house across the road there, the one with all the scrap vehicles and stuff out front and see if they can help us out."

"What am I asking for?"

"A hose clamp for Christs sakes! All we need is a bloody hose clamp. There's got to be something on one of those wrecks."

As Fooch starts walking he turns and shouts back, "There's no need for that kind of language. I have feelings you know."

Gill smiles, lights a cigarette and stares down at the problem.

As Fooch walks up the driveway to the house he gazes at all the stuff spread around the front and side yard. Several vehicles, whole and in part, discarded fridges, washing machines and the like. In the north, unlike near the big cities in the south, there are a lot of places like this. They're usually owned and occupied by older folks who are too old to work anymore and are just getting by on some sort of social assistance or pension. Most of these folks are decent people just wanting to live their remaining years in familiar surroundings. In most cases they'd give you the shirt off their back to help you.

Fooch approaches the front porch and see's an old timer sitting in a rocking chair having a coffee.

He eyes up Fooch for a moment.

"Looks like you guys have a bit of a problem. Rad or rad hose I'll bet."

As Fooch looks across the highway he can see Gill looking down under the hood. He turns to the old timer, "How the hell did you know that?"

"Used to be a mechanic. If it's the rad, I likely can't help but if it something minor like a hose or a clamp that's a different story."

"My buddy says it's just a clamp. Top rad hose clamp I think. We'd gladly pay you."

"Tell you buddy to come over. That white GMC over

there will have the clamp your looking for."

A short time later Gill crosses the highway and joins the two on the front porch.

The old timer asks, "Gill, is it? How the hell did you get a handle like that? Something to do with fishing I'll bet." He then quietly laughs.

"I have tools in that shed, you'll probably need a 3/16th or 8 mm wrench. Help yourself."

Gill heads into the shed, comes out with a handful of tools and heads back across the highway to the cube van. Twenty minutes later he returns with the broken hose clamp and shows it to the old guy named Mikey.

"Cheap crap they make nowadays. Go over to that white GMC truck there. You'll find one there. It's the same size."

Five minutes later Gill returns with the part, "It's a match. Should work fine."

"Your buddy here tells me you're a millwright. One of those jack of all trades and master of none guys. At least you have a clue how to fix things. Nowadays people just take it to the dealer. He also tells me you guys are hitchhiking to Edmonton. You ever considered the Greyhound?"

"What else has this wiener told you?" Gill takes the clamp and tools back across the highway.

After making the repair he returns, "Well that as they say is that."

Mikey gets the guys a coffee and the three sit on the porch shooting the shit for damn near an hour.

They find out that Mikey was born and raised in this house. He was a licensed mechanic working at the local service station for over 30 years. Around 10 years or so ago, the motel and small grocery store in the town closed. The service station was next. All throughout the north this type of thing is happening in these small towns. His wife passed a few years back, his son found work and lives in Sudbury now. He scrapes by on an old age pension and doing odd jobs and repairs for the locals.

Gill, "Sir, we can't thank you enough for your help. What do we owe you?"

Mikey says, "How about $10."

"Here's $20, please take it."

Mikey begrudgingly accepts, "Before you leave fill up that empty jug there with some water. You likely don't know how much antifreeze you lost. You know your real close to the turn off to our canyon. It would be worth your while to go have a look at it."

Back on the road again a few miles down the highway the guys take the short detour to see the famous Ouimet Canyon.

"My god Fooch, Mikey was right, just look at that. They say glaciers split open the earth's surface and over time erosion, water, wind and rain carved out the gorge."

Fooch just nods his head in agreement. After a few smokes, the guys are back on the road.

Gill, "Our delay back there only cost us a couple hours. With any luck, we should make Dryden before dark."

"You know Gill, I have to admit you were right about meeting new and interesting people on this adventure. Mikey seems to be happy. Other than his son being so far away he's exactly where he wants to be. In his house with his memories. It's not fancy. It's filled with useless stuff. But it's his useless stuff."

"Fooch the philosopher, I agree with you. Let's have a toast to Mikey."

Gill taps his coffee cup up against Fooch's brown bag containing his sherry.

As the cube van nears Thunder Bay they pass the Terry Fox monument crowded with people.

"That was a great man with a purpose. You know he met Bobby Orr."

Not much farther down the highway Fooch notices a sign Thunder Bay District Jail 1 km.

He pipes up, "Isn't that where they sent you and Doogy?"

"Yah yah, that was along time ago Fooch my old friend. Thanks for pointing that out."

"That wasn't one of your smarter moments, was it? It was in August 1969 as I recall. "

The event occurred over forty years ago in a small town near Hearst. It was during summer break. Gill, Fooch and at least six other good friends, all in their late teens, took their motorcycles north to visit and party with friends from this little town. One night Gill and his buddy Doogy went looking for some gas to borrow. They got caught, were charged and eventually convicted for theft under $50.

Gill shakes his head, "Yes it was the summer of 69. The famous church parking lot gasoline heist. Three dollars worth of gas stolen, three weeks in jail. A gross miscarriage of justice if you ask me. I must say though it was quite a learning experience.

That's a page in my book I won't forget. Dumbest thing I ever did."

After they pass Thunder Bay the cube van winds it's way through seemingly endless boreal forest for the next several hours.

Gill smiling, "What do you say Fooch, this is some way to hitchhike ehh?"

Fooch ignoring his friend rolls down his window and sticks his head out. He quickly brings it back inside.

"What's that smell, can't you smell that?"

"We must be getting near Dryden, that smell is coming from the big-ass pulp mill. They say you get used to it."

Soon they pull the cube van into a large truck stop close to the town of Dryden with a motel, restaurant/bar, etc.

"This place has everything we need. We'll crash here tonight. You know there's a 'Max the Moosefest' this weekend. Maybe we should hang around, party with the locals and get drunk."

"Where do you get all this useless information from? Who the hell is Max the moose?"

Gill explains, "Max is a huge statue of a moose erected back in the 60's as a tourist attraction I believe. You know the Dryden area has some of the best moose hunting in the north."

Sarcastically Fooch says, "Oh really, that's nice. We should stay then. Or not! You're an idiot. Here's a plan, lets get a room, get something to eat and have a few refreshments. We'll drink to Mikey and Max and bugger off in the morning."

"I like your plan oh wise one. Why didn't I think of that?"

"Because you're a dink that's why."

DAY NINE

Early next morning there's a light fog. The guys with only a mild hangover are having breakfast going over the days agenda.

"We're only a few hours from the Manitoba border. Southern Manitoba is only 400 some km wide, we'll make good time crossing it. We can then hop onto highway 16 and head towards Saskatoon. Maybe get as far as Yorkton. Oh, I phoned your pal Milty this morning, told him about the hose clamp problem and also found out how to get the van's damn CD player to work. We had the mode selector switch in the wrong position."

"What's with this we shit? You're a millwright, oh wise one, why couldn't you figure that out?"

Gill just shakes his head, "How about saying something like 'Thanks Gill ', now we can play our music. Sometimes I wonder why I even bother to talk to you, you turd. Let's go."

The guys are back on the road. The fog is starting to lift but still a concern. Patsy Cline is now playing on the CD player. Fooch's whining has stopped an all seems well. About 50 meters ahead Gill notices a dark object lumbering slowly onto the highway. A second later,

"Moose! Hang on!"

He piles on the brakes. Fooch nearly flies into the front windshield. His brown bag goes flying. The van screeches to a stop. A huge bull moose is six feet in front of the van. It stops, slowly turns its large rack laden head, looks at the guys as if to say, "You got a problem", then quietly finishes crossing the highway. After seconds of silence Gill manages to say, "That could have been interesting."

"Interesting? That's it! We damn near bought the farm and all you can say is that could have been interesting."

"Relax for Christ sake. Have a swig of your sherry, if you can find it. I'll find a place to pull over. I want to check the load in back."

"Good. Then you can check the load in back of my gitch."

Moments later the van is off the highway and Gill is in the back checking the Harleys.

"I have to tighten up some of these straps. This will take a few minutes. Why don't you go do something useful and change your underwear?"

Both men begin to laugh, "Well Fooch, this episode might become a page in your book ehh?"

"No shit Batman." More laughter, "I can't believe I just called you Batman. Sorry, asshole."

Some time later the guys, back on the road again, pass a huge roadside sign. 'Welcome to Manitoba'. The landscape is slowly changing. Still boreal forest but much less hilly. Tom Petty's 'Running Down a Dream' is playing. It's interesting how music from one's past can act almost as a drug creating a sense of contentment. They drive on. After they bypass Winnipeg they soon find themselves on highway 16 heading northwest towards Saskatoon making good time. They stop near a small town called Binscarth to have some supper and fuel up.

"Try this idea on for size Fooch. You drive this thing for the next few hours and let me rest. I'll then drive on until we're a few hours from Saskatoon. We can sleep in the van if we have to, carry on early in the morning and arrive early in Saskatoon. What do you say? Sound like a plan?"

Fooch, "Welllllll, as our old neighbour Gerry would say 'That's a farting good idea, why didn't I think of that?' You know that tiny little brain of yours never stops does it. One condition, I get to play my CD's, starting with Connie Francis then Brenda Lee and then some Johnny Cash."

Fooch gets behind the wheel checks the mirrors and gets comfortable.

"How are the brakes on this thing?"

They both laugh, "So Fooch, can you handle this thing?"

"Of course. I'm not just fog over here. Oh Gill, could you please slide in my Connie Francis CD? Thank you."

With his tunes playing and the late afternoon sun shining Fooch drives on for the next few hours. Gill, feet on the dash, is totally relaxed taking in the tunes.

Gill, "Man you gotta love Johnny Cash. Did I ever tell you my brother was at that concert, I think it was in Hamilton or maybe London when he proposed to June Carter on stage? That would have been cool. You know Fooch, at this moment all seems right with the world. I love you man."

"Why do you talk so stupid!"

"Seriously man I luvs you."

"You say that again and I'll put this thing in the ditch."

Gill continues looking out his window with a huge content smile on his face.

Many hours later after Gill has taken the wheel again, he pulls the van into a truck stop just before dark near a small town called "Dafoe". It's about two hours from Saskatoon.

"We've been driving for over twelve hours, this is far enough. Not a bad day ehh?"

"No not bad other than almost getting killed by a moose and me soiling myself, I'd give it a 6."

Fooch arranges an uncomfortable looking bed on the front seat while Gill crawls into the back with 'Harleys'.

DAY TEN

Next morning once again the guys are having breakfast in a truck stop diner. It's around 6 am.

Fooch, "Well oh wise one, what's your plan for today? Find a buffalo and run it over?"

Gill sarcastically smiles then offers up the days plan, "We deliver the bikes to the McCaffrey Farm, drop the van off in town, get back into our hitchhiking mode, by the way I have a terrific idea for a sign, then it's off to Edmonton. With any luck, we'll be at Nitty's for supper."

Fooch is looking into Gills ear, "You know I can almost see the tiny little gears turning in that tiny little brain of yours. What's this terrific idea for our sign?"

"It's a surprise. Finish your breaky and let's get going."

As planned the guys pull into the McCaffrey Farm around 9 am. A man in his 50's, likely the son is there to greet them.

"How was your trip? That's a long stretch. I talked to this 'Milty' fella yesterday, said you might get here today."

Gill recounts the moose excitement and after some small talk they unload the bikes.

"Man, those are two gorgeous Harleys. How's your dad doing?"

"Great, great, modern medicine you know. Two stints and he's as good as new. He can't wait till next year. We're going to try her again."

An hour later the guys drive through the city of Saskatoon and drop the van off at Milty's connection. Its location is in the north end of the city right on the main highway heading northwest to Lloydminster and then west to Edmonton. The guys setup on the side of the highway.

It's 11 am. Gill unveils his sign. 'Today Is Be Kind to Old Hichhikers Day.'

Fooch, "So this is your terrific idea? There's something seriously wrong with your head."

"Ok Fooch, oh ye of little faith, I'll bet you $10 we get picked up by noon."

"Make it $20 and you're on. This will be the easiest $20 I've ever made, oh ye with a tiny brain."

Not five minutes later a big grey sedan pulls over. A young man, in his 30's wearing a dress shirt, dress pants and sunglasses roles down his window. "Nice sign, where are you old timers headed?"

Gill, approaches the driver striding like a peacock, "We're headed to Edmonton sir. Anywhere close would be fine."

"Today's your lucky day, that's where I'm headed. Jump in."

After the guys load their gear in the backseat the driver asks, "Would you mind if one of you drive for awhile. I'm a little bushed."

"Sure, no problem." Gill gets behind the wheel with Fooch beside him up front while the young man crawls into the backseat and off they go.

Fooch asks, "Do you mind if we smoke?"

"Sure, why not."

It's not long before Gill notices the young man is sleeping in the back seat, "He wasn't shitting, he's bushed."

For the next few hours the guys are happily yakking and arguing about the last nine days, the people they've met, the shit that has happened. They also get into a discussion about their 'Wing' retirement home investment.

"You know Fooch, this 'Wing' thing is going to work, we're going to pull it off. Just think, in another ten or so years we'll be living with all our old buddies being looked after by a bunch of big busted blondes."

Fooch takes a hall from his bottle of sherry, "To the big busted blondes." They both laugh like a couple of school boys.

As they near the city of Lloydminster the young man in the back seat, who has been silent the whole time says, "There's a truck stop up there on the right, let's pull over and get some gas. I need to use the rest room."

Gill complies and pulls into the truck stop. The young man hands Gill $40. That should cover it."

The young man then heads to the rest room carrying a small shopping bag and back pack. Fooch heads to the diner to get a coffee for Gill. Gill gets $40 worth of gas. Ten minutes later the owner of the car emerges from the restroom wearing cut off jeans, a grey t-shirt, running shoes and his sunglasses. The three are back on the road again crossing into Alberta. Gill is still driving. Curiosity is getting the better of him.

"It's none of my business, by the way my names Gill and this is Fooch, but why the change of clothes?"

In the back seat the man is smiling, "I'm sorry fellas, you can call me Gary. I quit my job this morning. I've had it with my old way of life. I want no memories of it."

He leans back and lights up a smoke.

"Fair enough sir, don't mean to be nosey."

For the next while as before there's no conversation from Gary in the backseat.

As the three approach the outskirts of Edmonton Gill blurts out, "Hey, where's my $20! Come on pay up, you turd. By rights you should pay me double. It took less than five fricken minutes."

Fooch reaches into his shirt pocket grabs a crumpled up twenty and stuffs it under Gills collar.

Gill wiggles his neck a bit, "Oh yah that feels good."

Gary for the first time in hours joins the conversation, "What was the bet?"

Gill explains that his clever sign would get them picked up within the hour. And it did. Gary smiling, finishes his smoke, butts it out then flings it out the window.

"It did get my attention. And I figured you two old farts looked harmless enough. So, you two have hitched from southern Ontario all this way using this sign board. That's kinda clever."

Gill gloating now looks at Fooch points to his own head, "Kinda clever ehh."

Gary changes the subject, "Do you know where the Great Western Mall is? "

Gill, "Yah I think so, it's on 170th street, isn't it?"

"Correct, just stay on 16 and hang a left on 170. I'll show you where to turn. I have to meet a friend there."

"That's great. Our friend lives about ten minutes from that mall. Well Fooch, oh ye of little faith, won't Nitty be surprised to see us. We'll be there in time for supper."

They turn the grey sedan onto 170th street and head south. Ten minutes later around 5 pm, they turn into the Great Western Mall parking lot and park near one of the main busy entrances. This mall is huge. Hundreds of shops, a waterpark, a fun park for kids, it has everything.

Gary emerges from the backseat carrying a dull grey backpack, "Look fellas, I have to see my friend here, I'll be about ten minutes. Just wait here."

Thirty minutes later the guys, still out in the parking lot, are leaning on the trunk of the car.

Fooch, "Where the hell is this guy? What if he never comes out of there?"

"Don't worry he'll be out. Hell, if he doesn't come out soon we could walk to Nitty's from here."

They soon notice two police cars pull up close to the mall entrance. Several officers get out and quietly disperse.

Gill, "Hey, looks like something is going down. We have ring side seats. This could be interesting."

As the cops fan out, they appear to be forming a wide circle around our guys.

Fooch, "Gill, I don't like the look of this. What's going on here."

"How the hell should I know."

It soon becomes apparent the police are cautiously approaching on our guys and the grey sedan. Suddenly with guns drawn, a command comes from one of the officers, "Show us your hands!"

Totally in shock the guys comply and raise their hands, "Turn around slowly and put your hands on the car."

Again, they comply. Gill manages to whisper to Fooch, "It's gotta be that god damn Gary."

Several more cop cars arrive on scene. A crowd of curious onlookers is beginning to form with cell phones and cameras flashing. Tourists. Two officers cautiously approach and handcuff the guys leading them into the back of a black cruiser. Others begin to search the grey sedan bringing out the guys backpacks and sign board. The grey sedan is quickly cordoned off with crime scene tape.

In the front passenger seat of the black cruiser a large detective named Bill Hansen, a twenty-year veteran of the force asks for the guys ID.

As Gill and Fooch comply Gill asks, "Sir, would you mind telling us what the hell is going on here. This has to be a mistake."

The detective takes his time looking over the ID's, "So you claim to be Gerald Crest. Here's the situation Gerald. That grey sedan you're with was reported stolen around 10:45 am this morning in Saskatoon. A witness claims he saw a well dressed younger man taking it from a parking lot which coincidently happened to be near the scene of an armed bank robbery that had just occurred. A teller at the bank described the robber as a man in his 30's medium build and height, well dressed wearing sun glasses. We believe the man who robbed the bank also stole this grey sedan. It took us some time to make the connection. My question to you is why the hell are you two with this vehicle? What's your connection to this young man?"

Gill and Fooch look at each other in shock, "That son of a bitch Gary. Sir, the man your looking for is in the mall. He's wearing sun glasses a grey t-shirt, cut off jean shorts and old white running shoes. He's been in there for over 30 minutes now."

The detective picks up his radio and relays this info to the rest of his crew, "Get more officers down here and cover all the exits. He may still be in the mall."

You can see many of the officers at the scene quickly scramble off into the mall. The detective turns and continues to question the guys, "Can you describe this Gary? Facial features, hair color, that sort of thing."

Gill, "He has reddish blonde hair, never saw his eyes, he never took his sun glasses off, average build and height, nothing that stood out."

The detective quickly relays the suspects hair color to his team then returns his focus back to the guys.

"Tell me, why are you with this man? How do you know him? Does this Gary have a last name?"

"Sir, we don't know this guy from Adam. We were hitchhiking at the north end of Saskatoon around 11 am and this guy picked us up. That's it."

"You two were hitchhiking and he just picked you up? Really."

He turns, speaks to the other officer in the cruiser for a

moment then gets on his radio. "Captain, we're going to bring these two down to the station for questioning. We'll also impound the vehicle."

Gill, "What about our stuff?"

"Don't worry about your stuff, it's coming along. We're going to hold you two for awhile as persons of interest."

At the station Gill is alone in an interrogation room with two detectives across the table from him. One being Bill Hanson.

"Ok Gerald, tell us where you were and what you and your buddy did from the time you got up this morning."

Gill explains to the detectives they were doing a favour/job for a friend, Milty, driving a cube van from Marathon to Saskatoon delivering two motorcycles and that early this morning they drove from a town called Dafoe to the McCaffrey Farm near Saskatoon. They dropped off their cargo then they drove to the north end of the city and dropped off the cube van at Milty's business connection around 10:30 am. They then proceeded across the road from where they left the van and set up to hitchhike.

"Look, if you bring me my backpack I have a folder in there with all the names, addresses and phone numbers of these people and places."

Bill replies, "We found that and are currently checking it out. What was this man wearing?"

"A dress shirt, dress pants, nice shoes and sunglasses. Looked like a business man."

"You just told us he was wearing a grey t-shirt, cut off jeans and white running shoes. Is that correct?"

"Yes. You see, we pulled into that huge truck stop just outside Lloydminster for gas and stuff. He went into the restroom with his knapsack and changed his clothes."

"Did you not find that a little strange?"

Gill explains to detective Bill that he'd asked him about that and this Gary's reply was he quit his job that morning and wanted to forget about his old way of life.

Detective Bill, "But still, didn't that seem a bit strange to you? What did he do with his other clothes?"

"I did think it was odd at the time but after what we'd experienced on this trip so far it didn't seem that odd. I don't know what he did with his other clothes. Maybe he left them in the restroom at the truck stop. Hell, I don't know. It was none of our business. He gave us a ride."

Bill gets up and leaves the room, likely to get someone to check to see if the clothing was left at the truck stop in Lloydminster. The other detective holds up the guys white board sign. "Today Is Be Kind to Old Hichhikers Day".

"Would you mind explaining this? By the way you spelled hitch wrong."

As Gill again is explaining the sign and the reason for their trip Fooch is alone in a separate interrogation room. After being questioned by two other officers they both leave the room. Out in the observation area they can also see and hear the other interview taking place.

"These two don't look like bank robbers or even accomplices. As strange as their story is I think they're telling the truth. Who could make up a story like that?"

The other officer agrees, "Yah, but why would two old

farts want to hitch across the country?"

After Gill finishes his spiel to the other detective, detective Bill returns to the interrogation room.

"You say your destination is Edmonton. What's the reason for that again? Who were you planning on meeting?"

"Sir we planned a surprise visit to our old friend Nitty. If we ever get to see him he will be surprised, believe me."

"Why wouldn't you two fly out or take the bus? At your age don't you think its a little dangerous to hitch all that way?"

Gill shakes his head, "Oh Christ, not another one... Sorry Bill. I shouldn't have said that."

"Let me remind you this is some serious shit we're dealing with here. Alright Gerald, who is this friend of yours you were going to surprise and what's his address?"

Just then a female officer enters the room and hands Bill a folder.

As he's reading it Gill says, "His name is Allan Decker and he lives not ten minutes from that mall. Just check him out."

Bill's head snaps up, "Did you say Allan Decker?"

"Yes. We call him Nitty."

For the first time a smile appears on detective Bill's face. As he hands the folder to the other detective he pauses for a moment.

"Please don't tell me they call you Batman."

Gill (a.k.a. Gerald Crest a.k.a. Batman) is having another

one of those not knowing whether to shit or wind his watch moments.

"How, how the hell would you know that? What the hell's going on here?"

Both detectives get up and as they leave the room detective Bill says, "Just sit tight for awhile, we'll be back, in the meantime we'll have our sketch artist, Lindy, come in. Give her as much detail on the face of this Gary fella as you can."

After Lindy completes her sketch of this Gary character to the best of Gill's recollection she leaves the room, twenty minutes later Fooch is led into the room where Gill's been interrogated. He's totally beside himself. The two are now alone in the interrogation room.

"Well asshole, has this been interesting enough for you? We certainly have a ring side seat now you fricking genius! What the hell is happening?"

Gill is trying but failing to look relaxed and in control, "For Christ sake's man, both you and I know we had nothing to do with this thing. Don't worry."

Fooch almost screaming "Don't worry! Don't worry! Look where we are. You're the ex con, you're used to this."

"Ex con! What the hell are you talking about you idiot. I stole $3 worth of gas forty fucking years ago. Just relax."

The two bitch and whine back and forth over their situation. Meanwhile out in the observation area detective, Bill Hansen is with Allen Decker now, who they located and brought to the station rather quickly. They are watching the two with great amusement.

Allen, "Those are my buds alright. Listen to them. Bunch

of old ladies."

As it turns out Allen Decker (a.k.a. Nitty) and detective Bill have lived in the same neighbourhood for years. They frequent the same gym and have been good friends for years. After listening to the guys argue at each other they enter the interrogation room.

Nitty, "Holy fuck Batman, bank robbery! Grand theft auto! I thought I knew you two fools."

Gill and Fooch look at each other, see their buddy Nitty and together sarcastically reply, "Surprise!"

Nitty can no longer contain himself and burst out laughing. Detective Bill is also smiling and shaking his head.

Nitty, "I saw you two idiots on the local news not long ago being led into a cruiser. I thought I was seeing things. Bill here tells me you guys hitched all the way out here just to visit little old me. Isn't that nice. Why didn't you fly or take the bus?"

Gill just rolls his eyes, "Another one for gods sake."

Fooch almost shouting, "You want to know why we didn't fly out or take the bus? I'll tell you why. Because this genius thought it would be more fun to hitchhike. 'It'll be fun he said.' It'll be fun. "That's why. This isn't fun!"

Nitty points his finger at the two and starts laughing uncontrollably.

Detective Bill is smiling still shaking his head, "Your story checks out fellas. We're going to release you. I've been in this business for over twenty years and must say this is a first for me. Over the years, Allen here has told me stories about you two and to be honest I thought it was just exaggerated bullshit. I guess I was wrong. Look, we only ask you stay in town for a few days in case we find this Gary character. You're our best witnesses. Allen has offered to take you home with him. Please accept. I'm sure you'll have lots to talk about."

CONCLUSION

That was pretty much the end of our little excursion across the country. Fooch and I spent the next several days with our friend Nitty catching up and describing, in great detail, our adventure. Alcohol was involved. The police never found the bank robber/car thief known only as Gary. Ironically, we then flew home much to the delight of Fooch, who hates flying.

So, back to the beginning of the story. You ask, what's this unusual letter I just received have to do with this adventure of ours? After I read it to you I want you to ask yourself, if you were me, what would you do with this letter?

Here's what it says. "Dear Gerald, I want to apologize for the situation I left you and your buddy in back in the parking lot of The Great Western Mall. I thought you guys would have got tired of waiting for me to return and just leave. I never dreamt the police would find the stolen car that fast. For that I'm sorry. You probably think of me as just a selfish criminal who cares only about himself, but I must explain something to you. While we were driving across Saskatchewan I listened from the backseat to you and your buddy talking for hours about your crazy trip, about meeting new people, and about your 'Wing' retirement plan. I remember you saying how important it will be to spend your waning years with old friends in your 'Wing'. Truer words were never spoken. All I will say is the money I stole was not for myself but for someone I care deeply about and leave it at that. Good luck with your 'Wing'. I think it's a fantastic idea."

I want to believe there's good in everyone. Even this Gary character, if that's his name. Why would this guy risk sending me this letter unless he's telling the truth? Am I fooling myself? Should I give it to the police? He at least has a conscience. Hell I don't know. I'm going to file the contents of this letter in my 'Book of Life' along a few new pages from our recent adventure.

As for the physical letter itself, mister zippo here is taking care of that right now. Don't you just love the smell from a zippo lighter being lit and burning paper?

THE END.

Manufactured by Amazon.ca
Bolton, ON